THE ATLANTA BRAVES

BY
MARK STEWART

NORWOOD HOUSE PRESS
CHICAGO, ILLINOIS

Norwood House Press
P.O. Box 316598
Chicago, Illinois 60631

For information regarding Norwood House Press, please visit our website at:
www.norwoodhousepress.com or call 866-565-2900.

All photos courtesy of Getty Images except the following:
SportsChrome (4, 11, 23, 37, 40), Allen & Ginter's (6), American Tobacco (7), Macfadden Publications (9),
Black Book Partners Archives (10, 11, 25), Tom DiPace (14, 31), Golden Books (15),
Topps, Inc. (21, 22, 30, 35 top left and bottom, 39, 43 both, 45), F.W. Rueckheim & Brother (24),
Baseball Magazine (28), Author's Collection (33, 34 all), Old Judge & Gypsy Queen (36),
Street & Smith (38), Bowman Gum Co. (41), Sportfolio (42 top),
Classic Games (42 bottom), Matt Richman (48).
Cover Photo: Scott Cunningham/Getty Images

The memorabilia and artifacts pictured in this book are presented for educational and informational purposes,
and come from the collection of the author.

Editor: Mike Kennedy
Designer: Ron Jaffe
Project Management: Black Book Partners, LLC.
Special thanks to Topps, Inc.

Library of Congress Cataloging-in-Publication Data

Stewart, Mark, 1960-
  The Atlanta Braves / by Mark Stewart.
    p. cm. -- (Team spirit)
  Includes bibliographical references and index.
  Summary: "A Team Spirit Baseball edition featuring the Atlanta Braves that
chronicles the history and accomplishments of the team. Includes access to
the Team Spirit website, which provides additional information, updates and
photos"--Provided by publisher.
  ISBN 978-1-59953-473-2 (library edition : alk. paper) -- ISBN
978-1-60357-353-5 (ebook) 1. Atlanta Braves (Baseball
team)--History--Juvenile literature. I. Title.
  GV875.A8S83 2012
  796.357'6409758231--dc23
                                                    2011047940

Manufactured in the United States of America in North Mankato, Minnesota.
196N—012012

COVER PHOTO: The Braves celebrate a win in 2011.

TABLE OF CONTENTS

ABOUT OUR GLOSSARY

In this book, there may be several words that you are reading for the first time. Some are sports words, some are new vocabulary words, and some are familiar words that are used in an unusual way. All of these words are defined on page 46. Throughout the book, sports words appear in **bold type**. Regular vocabulary words appear in ***bold italic type***.

MEET THE BRAVES

Building a winning baseball team takes a lot of time and money. Few clubs have done it better than the Atlanta Braves. Year in and year out, they put good players on the field. Some are stars and some are not. When they play together as a team, however, the result is usually a victory.

The Braves have built their winning *tradition* over the course of many *decades*. In fact, they have been playing baseball longer than any other team. During this time, fans in the Northeast, Midwest, and South have called the Braves their own. The club has been the champion of baseball at each stop.

This book tells the story of the Braves. They are an easy team to root for, because they play the game well and have fun doing it. Atlanta's players may be grownups, but there is still a lot of kid in all of them.

Tim Hudson shares a laugh with catcher Brian McCann on the pitcher's mound during a 2011 game.

GLORY DAYS

T he Braves have called three cities home. The team started in Boston, Massachusetts as the Red Stockings in 1871, in the earliest days of professional baseball. More than 50 years would pass before fans started calling them the Braves. In 1876, Boston was one of eight cities that formed the **National League (NL)**. The team changed its name to Red Caps that season.

JOHN CLARKSON.
ALLEN & GINTER'S
RICHMOND. *Cigarettes*. VIRGINIA.

The Red Caps had many of the best players in baseball, including Deacon White, Jim O'Rourke, and Tommy Bond. The team's manager was Harry Wright. His brother, George, played shortstop for the Red Caps.

In the 1880s, the club became the Beaneaters. A new group of stars led this team, including Hugh Duffy, Tommy McCarthy, Bobby Lowe, Mike "King" Kelly, John Clarkson, and Kid Nichols. Each is now in the **Hall of Fame**. In all, Boston won the NL **pennant** eight times during the 1800s.

LEFT: John Clarkson won 149 games in five seasons for Boston. **RIGHT**: This card of David Shean from 1911 shows the team name as Rustlers.

By the early 1900s, the team's stars had all retired. Boston struggled to win without them and went many years without a *competitive* club. The Beaneaters tried everything to reverse their fortunes. They even changed their name—three times!—first to the Nationals, then to the Doves, and finally to the Rustlers. Nothing worked.

In 1912, the team changed its name again, this time to the Braves. Two years later, Boston found itself in last place in the middle of July. Then something wonderful happened. The Braves got hot and rose in the standings. They were baseball's best team by the end of the season and won their first **World Series**. The Braves went 34 years before they reached the World Series again. In 1948, Boston faced the Cleveland Indians but lost in six games.

Five years later, the Braves made headlines off the field. From 1901 to 1952, they had shared Boston with another team, the Red Sox. Unfortunately, there were not enough baseball fans in the city to support both clubs. The Braves moved to Milwaukee, Wisconsin in 1953. It was the first time a baseball team had changed cities in 50 years.

Baseball fans in Milwaukee came out to see the Braves by the millions. The Braves gave

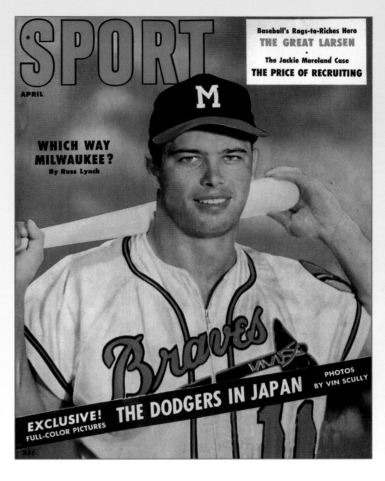

them plenty of thrills. The team had a good mix of young stars led by Hank Aaron and Eddie Mathews. Older players such as Warren Spahn and Andy Pafko added experience to the roster. The Braves rewarded their fans by winning the pennant twice and claiming their second World Series championship in 1957.

LEFT: Hank Aaron was the NL's top player in 1957, the same year he led the Braves to a World Series championship.   **ABOVE**: Eddie Mathews teamed with Aaron to give the Braves two great sluggers.

In 1966, the Braves decided to move again. This time they went south to Atlanta, Georgia. At the time, there were no **big-league** teams in the Southeast. The Braves found millions of loyal, baseball-hungry fans in this part of the country. In just their fourth season in Atlanta, the Braves finished first in the **NL West**.

Over the next four decades, the Braves became one of the best teams in baseball. They won the **NL East** 15 times, captured five pennants, and won a third World Series championship, in 1995. The Braves developed excellent power hitters, including Dale Murphy, Dave Justice, Ryan Klesko, Javy Lopez, Andruw Jones, and Chipper Jones. Atlanta's pitching was even better. Tom Glavine, John Smoltz, and Greg Maddux led the way beginning in the 1990s.

During the early years of the 21st century, the Braves turned to new players to **sustain** their winning tradition. Players such as Chipper Jones and Smoltz taught a new **generation** how the "old-timers" got it done. The success continued, thanks to young stars such as Tim Hudson, Brian McCann, Jair Jurrjens, Martin Prado, Freddie Freeman, Jason Heyward, and Craig Kimbrel. Although the Braves had a lot of new faces, they won in familiar ways—timely hitting, good fielding, smart baserunning, and pitching that just won't quit.

HOME TURF

The Braves play in Turner Field, which is located a few minutes from downtown Atlanta. The stadium has the spirit of an old-time ballpark, even though it was built in the 1990s. It was finished in time for the *Summer Olympics* of 1996, and the Braves moved in at the start of the 1997 season.

The Braves' stadium was built next to Fulton County Stadium, the team's home from 1966 to 1996. The site of the old park is now a parking lot, but the bases are still marked out on the blacktop. There are many popular stops inside the new stadium, including the Braves Hall of Fame and Monument Grove. The first thing that most fans notice when they reach their seats is a Coke bottle out behind the outfield fence that stands 38 feet tall.

BY THE NUMBERS

- The Braves' stadium has 49,586 seats.
- The distance from home plate to the left field foul pole is 335 feet.
- The distance from home plate to the center field fence is 401 feet.
- The distance from home plate to the right field foul pole is 330 feet.

Atlanta's stadium is nearly full for a game during the 2007 season.

DRESSED FOR SUCCESS

The Braves have used deep red and blue in their uniforms since 1946. That season, the team began wearing its famous script *Braves* design. During the 1970s, the club switched to bright uniforms that had a more modern look. By the end of the 1980s, the team had returned to its old uniform style.

JOE ADCOCK

From 1936 to 1940, the Braves were known as the Bees. During that time, the team colors were dark blue and gold, which made the players look a little like bees. Still, many fans kept calling them by their old name. They were happy when the team became the Braves again in 1941.

The team's **logo** features *Braves* written in script above a tomahawk. For many years, the club used a smiling Native American. Many people thought that was disrespectful, so the Braves eventually made a change.

LEFT: Craig Kimbrel delivers a pitch in the team's 2011 home uniform.
ABOVE: Joe Adcock's uniform in this 1954 sticker looks similar to Kimbrel's.

The Braves' winning tradition is much older than most fans imagine. The team captured championships in the 1870s, 1880s, and 1890s. In 1892, the Boston Beaneaters were the first club ever

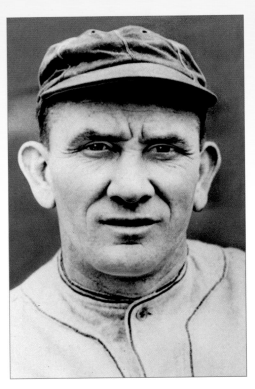

to win 100 games in a season. That team won with great pitching, smart baserunning, good hitting, and steady fielding. Hugh Duffy and Herman Long were the Beaneaters' top hitters. Pitchers Kid Nichols and Jack Stivetts won 35 games each.

No one expected that kind of performance from the 1914 Braves. They were in last place on July 18 that season, with the New York Giants far out in front. Then something magical happened. Boston could not lose. Manager George Stallings made all the right calls from the dugout. Rabbit Maranville and Johnny Evers gave the team a spark

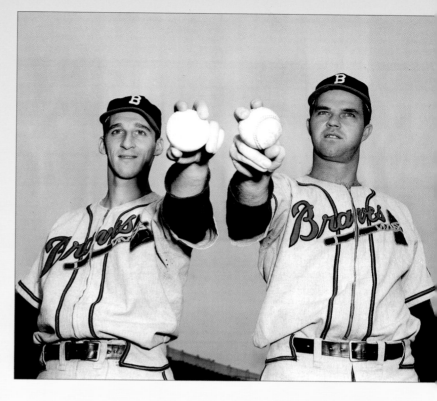

LEFT: Rabbit Maranville
RIGHT: Warren Spahn and Johnny Sain won nine games for the Braves in the final weeks of the 1948 season.

every game. The Braves not only caught the Giants—they finished more than 10 games ahead! In the World Series, Boston continued its amazing play and beat the Philadelphia A's four games to none. This team is called the "Miracle Braves" to this day.

The Braves did not win another World Series during their time in Boston. However, in 1948, they surprised baseball fans again by winning another exciting pennant. The Braves found themselves in a four-way battle for first place in the season's final month. With pitchers Warren Spahn and Johnny Sain leading the way, they won 14 of 15 games to finish far ahead of the other teams.

During their 13 years in Milwaukee, the Braves won the World Series once, in 1957. That fall, they faced the New York Yankees. Fans were on the edge of their seats in every game.

Lew Burdette took the mound for the Braves in Game 7 in New York. Milwaukee scored four runs in the third inning, and Burdette took over from there. He threw his second **shutout** in a row to give the Braves their first championship since 1914.

Hank Aaron was the hitting star for the Braves. He batted .393 and smacked three home runs. But nobody was better than Burdette. He won three games and gave up only two runs the entire series. He was an easy pick as the **Most Valuable Player (MVP)**.

After moving to Atlanta, the Braves waited until 1995 before they were champions again. The team had a great season from start to finish. In the World Series, the Braves played the Cleveland Indians. Atlanta had relied on great pitching and timely hitting all year long. The team used the same formula to beat the Indians.

Greg Maddux pitched the Braves to a 3–2 victory in Game 1. Tom Glavine was just as good the next day, and Atlanta won again. Manager Bobby Cox handed the ball to Glavine again for Game 6 at home. The Indians got just one hit off him. Dave Justice broke a 0–0 tie in the sixth inning with a home run. Mark Wohlers finished off Cleveland in the ninth inning. The Braves celebrated their third championship with their fans in Atlanta.

LEFT: The Braves celebrate their victory over the Yankees in 1957.
RIGHT: Mark Wohlers jumps for joy after pitching the Braves to the 1995 pennant.

Go-To Guys

To be a true star in baseball, you need more than a quick bat and a strong arm. You have to be a "go-to guy"—someone the manager wants on the pitcher's mound or in the batter's box when it matters most. Fans of the Braves have had a lot to cheer about over the years, including these great stars …

THE PIONEERS

KING KELLY   Outfielder/Catcher

- BORN: 12/31/1857 • DIED: 11/8/1894
- PLAYED FOR TEAM: 1887 TO 1889 & 1891 TO 1892

King Kelly was the most popular player the team ever had while it played in Boston. He was the game's most daring runner. Whenever he was on the basepaths, the fans would yell, "Slide, Kelly, slide!"

HUGH DUFFY   Outfielder

- BORN: 11/26/1866 • DIED: 10/19/1954 • PLAYED FOR TEAM: 1892 TO 1900

Hugh Duffy was the best hitter on the Boston teams of the 1890s. In 1894, he became the first batter to win the **Triple Crown**. Duffy's batting average of .438 that year is still the highest in history.

RIGHT: Del Crandall

WARREN SPAHN   Pitcher

- BORN: 4/23/1921   • DIED: 11/24/2003
- PLAYED FOR TEAM: 1942 & 1946 TO 1964

Warren Spahn was the Braves' best pitcher for more than 15 years. He had a good fastball and could also throw pitches that broke left or right. Spahn won 363 games—more than any left-handed pitcher in history.

DEL CRANDALL   Catcher

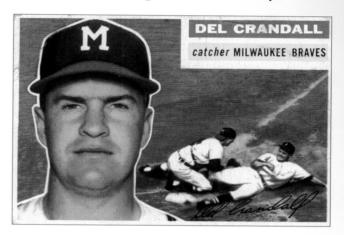

- BORN: 3/5/1930
- PLAYED FOR TEAM: 1949 TO 1963

Del Crandall was a genius when it came to calling for the right pitch at the right time. Crandall was an **All-Star** 11 times and won four **Gold Gloves**.

EDDIE MATHEWS   Third Baseman

- BORN: 10/13/1931   • DIED: 2/18/2001   • PLAYED FOR TEAM: 1952 TO 1966

Eddie Mathews was the best fielder and hitter at his position for 10 years. He had one of the fastest swings in history. Mathews was the only man to play for the Braves in Boston, Milwaukee, and Atlanta.

HANK AARON   Outfielder

- BORN: 2/5/1934   • PLAYED FOR TEAM: 1954 TO 1974

Hank Aaron smashed line drives all over the field. He was an All-Star in 20 of his 21 years with the Braves. In 1974, Aaron became baseball's all-time home run king. Barry Bonds broke his record in 2007.

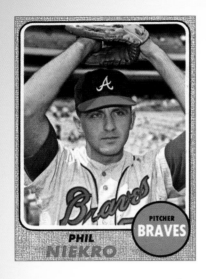

PHIL
NIEKRO

PHIL NIEKRO   Pitcher

• BORN: 4/1/1939   • PLAYED FOR TEAM: 1964 TO 1983 & 1987

Phil Niekro won more than 300 games using a **knuckleball**. This tricky pitch often moved just as the batter was swinging. Niekro was beloved by the people of Atlanta for his loyalty to the Braves.

DALE MURPHY   Outfielder

• BORN: 3/12/1956   • PLAYED FOR TEAM: 1976 TO 1990

Dale Murphy was a powerful hitter, fast runner, and graceful fielder. When Murphy retired, he had played more games in an Atlanta uniform than any other player.

TOM GLAVINE   Pitcher

• BORN: 3/25/1966 • PLAYED FOR TEAM: 1987 TO 2002 & 2008

Tom Glavine was Atlanta's best left-handed pitcher during the 1990s. He had pinpoint control and almost never gave a batter a good pitch to hit. Glavine won the **Cy Young Award** in 1991 and again in 1998.

JOHN SMOLTZ   Pitcher

• BORN: 5/15/1967   • PLAYED FOR TEAM: 1988 TO 2008

The more pressure John Smoltz felt, the better he threw. After winning more than 150 games as a starting pitcher, Smoltz became a relief pitcher for four years and had more than 150 **saves**.

GREG MADDUX   Pitcher

- BORN: 4/14/1966
- PLAYED FOR TEAM: 1993 TO 2003

Greg Maddux did some of the finest pitching ever during his 11 years with the Braves. At a time when home runs were being hit in record numbers, it was very difficult to score a run against him.

CHIPPER JONES   Third Baseman

- BORN: 4/24/1972
- FIRST YEAR WITH TEAM: 1993

Chipper Jones was one of baseball's best **switch-hitters**. He had 100 or more **runs batted in (RBIs)** eight years in a row. Jones was named the NL MVP in 1999.

BRIAN McCANN   Catcher

- BORN: 2/20/1984
- FIRST YEAR WITH TEAM: 2005

Brian McCann was a powerful hitter who also played great defense behind home plate. He was an All-Star in each of his first six full seasons.

LEFT: Phil Niekro   **RIGHT**: Greg Maddux

CALLING THE SHOTS

When the Braves were called the Boston Red Caps, they had baseball's first true manager. His name was Harry Wright, and he was a baseball pioneer. Wright discussed *strategy* with his players and ran organized practices. Frank Selee followed Wright. He was known for taking young players and moving them to new positions. Many of these players ended up in the Hall of Fame.

STALLINGS, BOSTON - NATIONALS

Three managers have each won a World Series with the Braves: George Stallings, Fred Haney, and Bobby Cox. Stallings found clever ways to get the most out of his teams. He was one of the first managers to **platoon** two players at the same position. Haney led the Braves to the pennant in 1957 and 1958. He worked his players hard. "You may hate me in the spring," he told them, "but you'll love me in the fall, when you pick up your World Series checks!"

LEFT: George Stallings was the first Braves manager to win the World Series. **RIGHT**: Bobby Cox was named Manager of the Year twice.

Cox was by far the team's most successful manager. No matter what kind of team he had, Cox always found a way to win. He was not afraid to give young players a chance. He trusted his coaches to teach them the right way to play baseball. Cox first managed the Braves from 1978 to 1981. It was his idea to move Dale Murphy from catcher to the outfield. After the switch, Murphy became the NL MVP—twice!

Cox returned to the Atlanta dugout in 1990. The following season, the Braves reached the World Series. In 1995, they took the championship. Under Cox, the team finished first in the NL East 14 times and won the pennant five times. He was named Manager of the Year in 2004 and 2005. No one had ever won this award twice in a row.

ONE GREAT DAY

For as long as anyone could remember, the most famous record in sports belonged to Babe Ruth. He hit 714 home runs in his career. No one came close to breaking Ruth's record until Hank Aaron in the 1970s. With each home run Aaron hit, he crept closer and closer to 714. By the end of the 1973 season, Aaron had 713.

That winter, Aaron was the most famous man in America. Newspaper writers and television cameras followed him everywhere he went. He also received hate mail from racists who did not want an African-American to break Ruth's record. There was so much pressure! By the time the 1974 season started, Aaron just wanted to hit numbers 714 and 715—so that everyone would leave him alone. His greatest fear was that it might take several weeks, and that the pressure would keep building.

Aaron made every swing count. He hit his 714th home run on Opening Day in Cincinnati against the Reds. This set the stage

Hank Aaron shows his record-breaking home run ball to the crowd.

for his historic home run when the Braves went back home to Atlanta.

The Braves played the Los Angeles Dodgers, with millions of fans watching the game on television. Aaron stepped to the plate in the fourth inning against Al Downing. He waited for the left-hander to make a mistake. When Aaron saw a pitch that was right down the middle, he whipped his bat around and hit a long drive to left field. The ball cleared the fence for number 715. As he trotted around the bases, Aaron cracked a big smile. He was proud to be baseball's new home run king—and happy to get it over with!

LEGEND HAS IT

ABOVE: Bama Rowell

WHICH BRAVE INSPIRED THE WRITER OF A FAMOUS BASEBALL BOOK?

LEGEND HAS IT that Bama Rowell did. In 1946, Rowell hit a long home run that broke the large clock at Brooklyn's Ebbets Field. Pieces of glass rained down on the outfield. Author Bernard Malamud was at the game. In Malamud's novel *The Natural*, the hero wins the pennant with a home run that crashes into a light tower and showers the field with sparks and glass.

WHICH BRAVE HAD FOUR HOMERS GO TO WASTE?

LEGEND HAS IT that Bob Horner did. It is rare for a player to hit four home runs in one game. It is even more rare when he does this and his team loses. In a 1986 game against the Montreal Expos, Horner hit three home runs off Andy McGaffigan and a fourth against Jeff Reardon. The Expos won the game 11–8. Horner was the first player in 90 years to hit four home runs in a loss.

WHICH BRAVE SIMPLY REFUSED TO LOSE?

LEGEND HAS IT that Joe Oeschger did. The Braves have had many competitive players over the years. However, none was put to the test like Oeschger. In a 1919 game against the Philadelphia Phillies, he pitched all 20 innings in a 9–9 tie. In a 1920 game against the Brooklyn Dodgers, Oeschger pitched all 26 innings in a 1–1 tie. The umpires called both games because it got too dark to see. Oeschger and his Brooklyn opponent, Leon Cadore, still share the record for most innings pitched in a game.

Braves fans will forever remember 2011 as a season of streaks. Dan Uggla, Freddie Freeman, and Craig Kimbrel will remember it that way, too. Each of them put together an amazing stretch of games during the year.

Uggla's streak could not have come at a better time. Halfway through the season, fans in Atlanta were almost ready to give up on him. Uggla was the team's new second baseman. He was having a terrible year. Uggla was batting just .174 through the first three months. In early July, he got two hits against the Colorado Rockies. He got two more the next day. The next time Uggla went hitless was August 14. In all, he had one or more hits in 33 games in a row.

During Uggla's streak, Freeman also got in a groove. He batted safely in 20 games in a row. That made Uggla and Freeman the

first teammates in more than a century to have 20-game hitting streaks at the same time.

Meanwhile, Kimbrel was also streaking—on the mound. On June 14, he pitched a scoreless inning against the New York Mets. Kimbrel didn't give up a run in his next 37 appearances. His streak lasted through July and August. It finally ended against the St. Louis Cardinals in early September. In all, Kimbrel pitched more than 37 innings without allowing a run. During that time, he won two games and saved 25. Kimbrel finished the year with 46 saves, which set a new record for a first-year pitcher. A few months later, he was named **Rookie of the Year**.

TEAM SPIRIT

Atlanta is a patriotic city. Wherever you go, you are likely to see a lot of red, white, and blue. When the Braves are in town, those colors are everywhere. Fans love to show off their caps, jackets, jerseys, pennants, and pins. At Braves games, they sometimes go a little overboard. But that's what great fans do.

Because of the support they get from their fans, the Braves really enjoy playing in Atlanta. They know that the fans appreciate a well-played game. In fact, the crowds at the Braves' stadium cheer just as loudly for stolen bases and double plays as they do for home runs. The people who root for the Braves have seen a lot of winning over the years. They understand that the "little things" often make the difference between victory and defeat.

LEFT: Atlanta fans love their Braves and are proud to show it.
ABOVE: Milwaukee fans loved the Braves as much as the people of Atlanta do. They celebrated their 1958 NL championship with this souvenir pennant.

TIMELINE

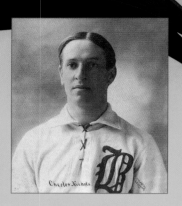

Kid Nichols

1871
The team goes 22–10 in its first season.

1893
Kid Nichols pitches the team to its third pennant in a row.

1936
The team changes its name to Bees.

1876
Boston plays the first game in NL history.

1914
The Braves win the World Series.

HARRY WRIGHT

Harry Wright was the manager of the team in 1876.

Bill James won two games in the 1914 World Series.

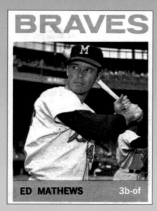

BRAVES

ED MATHEWS   3b-of

Eddie Mathews was the hitting star of the 1953 Braves.

Javy Lopez hits a World Series home run in 1995.

1953
The Braves move to Milwaukee.

1966
The Braves move to Atlanta.

1995
The Braves win the World Series.

1957
The Braves win the World Series.

1974
Hank Aaron becomes baseball's all-time home run king.

2011
Craig Kimbrel sets a rookie record with 46 saves.

Lew Burdette, Warren Spahn, and Bob Buhl combined for 56 wins in 1957.

MOUND MAGICIANS

BURDETTE—SPAHN—BUHL

FUN FACTS

LOWE BLOWS

In 1894, Bobby Lowe became the first big leaguer to hit four home runs in a game. He hit two in the third inning. After the game, Boston fans "passed the hat" and filled it with more than $150 for Lowe.

STAR POWER

King Kelly was the first player to sign autographs for fans. In 1891, the song "Slide, Kelly, Slide" became one of the first songs recorded for sale to the public.

BYE-BYE, BABE

Home run champion Babe Ruth played his last season in 1935 as a member of the Braves. He hit his final three home runs in one game against the Pittsburgh Pirates. One ball flew entirely out of the stadium.

NICE START, KID

In 2010, 20-year-old Jason Heyward hit a home run in his first trip to the plate as a big leaguer. Only two players in history have done this at a younger age.

MR. MILESTONE

In 2011, Chipper Jones got his 500th double, 1,500th RBI, and 2,500th hit. He finished the season as the only switch-hitter with more than 400 home runs and a lifetime average over .300.

CLEARING THE BASES

In 1966, Tony Cloninger set a record when he hit two **grand slams** for the Braves in one game. He was not a power hitter—he was a pitcher!

BRAVE NEW WORLD

In 1914, Cuban star Adolfo Luque of the Braves became the first Latino ever to pitch in the big leagues.

LEFT: King Kelly   **ABOVE**: Chipper Jones

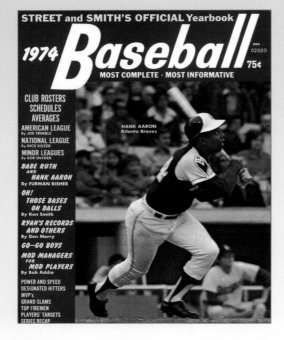

STREET and SMITH'S OFFICIAL Yearbook

1974 *Baseball* 75¢
ccc
02050

MOST COMPLETE · MOST INFORMATIVE

CLUB ROSTERS
SCHEDULES
AVERAGES
AMERICAN LEAGUE
By JOE TRIMBLE
NATIONAL LEAGUE
By DICK DOZER
MINOR LEAGUES
By BOB SNYDER
BABE RUTH
AND
HANK AARON
By FURMAN BISHER
OH!
THOSE BASES
ON BALLS
By Ken Smith
RYAN'S RECORDS
AND OTHERS
By Don Merry
GO—GO BOYS
MOD MANAGERS
FOR
MOD PLAYERS
By Bob Addie
POWER AND SPEED
DESIGNATED HITTERS
MVP's
GRAND SLAMS
TOP FIREMEN
PLAYERS' TARGETS
SERIES RECAP

HANK AARON
Atlanta Braves

"I never smile when I have a bat in my hands. That's when you've got to be serious."

▶ **HANK AARON**, ON WHAT MADE HIM ONE OF BASEBALL'S MOST DANGEROUS HITTERS

"Ever since I was a little kid, the last thing I wanted to do was lose. I hated losing. I still hate it."

▶ **TIM HUDSON**, ON WHAT DRIVES HIM

"Hitting is timing. Pitching is upsetting timing."

▶ **WARREN SPAHN**, ON THE SECRET TO BEING A GOOD PITCHER

"You don't have to get hits to impress the manager."

▶ **BOBBY COX**, ON PLAYERS WHO DO THE LITTLE THINGS THAT WIN GAMES

"I take the mound with the focus that we can't lose. I don't know any other way to do it."

▶ *JOHN SMOLTZ, ON WHAT MADE HIM TO HARD TO BEAT*

"My mother used to pitch to me and my father would **shag** balls. If I hit one up the middle close to my mother, I'd have some extra chores to do."

▶ *EDDIE MATHEWS, ON HOW HE LEARNED TO HIT THE BALL TO LEFT FIELD*

"This was one of the greatest moments in my life, one I wanted to cherish and stretch out forever."

▶ *TOM GLAVINE, ON WINNING THE WORLD SERIES WITH THE BRAVES IN 1995*

TOM GLAVINE

LEFT: Hank Aaron
RIGHT: Tom Glavine

GREAT DEBATES

eople who root for the Braves love to compare their favorite moments, teams, and players. Some debates have been going on for years! How would you settle these classic baseball arguments?

THE 1995 BRAVES WERE THE BEST IN TEAM HISTORY ...

… because they won the NL East by 21 games that year. The Braves lost once in the **playoffs** before reaching the World Series. Then they beat the Cleveland Indians in six games. Atlanta had seven power hitters in its batting order and three of baseball's best pitchers in Greg Maddux, Tom Glavine, and John Smoltz. The Braves also had Bobby Cox, the best manager in the game.

BUHL

LET'S JUST SAY THE 1995 BRAVES WERE THE BEST ATLANTA TEAM ...

… because the 1957 Milwaukee Braves would have destroyed them. Warren Spahn, Lew Burdette, and Bob Buhl (LEFT) were every bit as good Maddux, Glavine, and Smoltz. In fact, they won nine more games than those guys. Hank Aaron and Eddie Mathews hit 76 home runs in 1957—and a total of 863 as teammates. One more thing: The Braves won the World Series against the mighty New York Yankees—which wasn't an easy thing to do!

JOHN SMOLTZ WAS THE GREATEST PITCHER IN TEAM HISTORY ...

... because when the Braves were playing for a championship, he was at his best. Smoltz's record in the playoffs and World Series was 15–4. At age 24, Smoltz (RIGHT) threw a shutout in Game 7 of the 1991 NLCS. Fourteen years later, in his final playoff game as a Brave, he beat the Houston Astros 7–1.

GREG MADDUX AND WARREN SPAHN MIGHT HAVE SOMETHING TO SAY ABOUT THAT ...

... because their numbers blow Smoltz's away. Maddux won the Cy Young Award in his first three seasons with Atlanta and earned 10 Gold Gloves in a row. Spahn won 356 games for the Braves. He led the NL in victories eight times and in **complete games** nine times. Spahn also hit 35 homers as a batter!

FOR THE RECORD

T he great Braves teams and players have left their marks on the record books. These are the "best of the best" ...

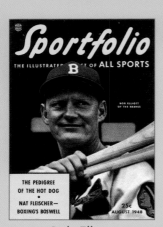

Bob Elliott

Dave Justice

BRAVES AWARD WINNERS

WINNER	AWARD	YEAR
Bob Elliott	Most Valuable Player	1947
Sam Jethroe	Rookie of the Year	1950
Hank Aaron	Most Valuable Player	1957
Warren Spahn	Cy Young Award	1957
Earl Williams	Rookie of the Year	1971
Bob Horner	Rookie of the Year	1978
Dale Murphy	Most Valuable Player	1982
Dale Murphy	Most Valuable Player	1983
Dave Justice	Rookie of the Year	1990
Terry Pendleton	Most Valuable Player	1991
Tom Glavine	Cy Young Award	1991
Greg Maddux	Cy Young Award	1993
Greg Maddux	Cy Young Award	1994
Greg Maddux	Cy Young Award	1995
John Smoltz	Cy Young Award	1996
Tom Glavine	Cy Young Award	1998
Chipper Jones	Most Valuable Player	1999
Rafael Furcal	Rookie of the Year	2000
Bobby Cox	Manager of the Year	2004
Bobby Cox	Manager of the Year	2005
Brian McCann	All-Star Game MVP	2010
Craig Kimbrel	Rookie of the Year	2011

BRAVES ACHIEVEMENTS

ACHIEVEMENT	YEAR
National Association Pennant	1872*
National Association Pennant	1873
National Association Pennant	1874
National Association Pennant	1875
NL Pennant Winner	1877
NL Pennant Winner	1878
NL Pennant Winner	1883
NL Pennant Winner	1891
NL Pennant Winner	1892
NL Pennant Winner	1893
NL Pennant Winner	1897
NL Pennant Winner	1898
NL Pennant Winner	1914
World Series Champions	1914
NL Pennant Winner	1948
NL Pennant Winner	1957
World Series Champions	1957
NL Pennant Winner	1958
NL Pennant Winner	1991
NL Pennant Winner	1992
NL Pennant Winner	1995
World Series Champions	1995
NL Pennant Winner	1996
NL Pennant Winner	1999

The National Association was the first professional baseball league. It lasted from 1871 to 1875.

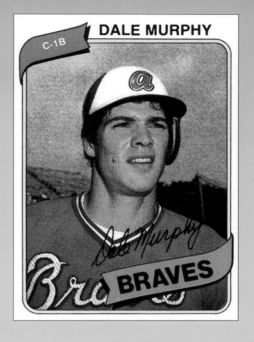

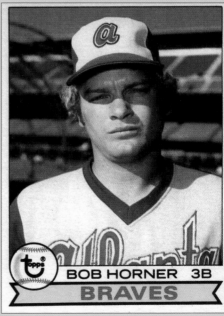

TOP RIGHT: Dale Murphy was the MVP in 1982 and 1983.
BOTTOM RIGHT: Bob Horner was the league's best rookie in 1978.

PINPOINTS

T he history of a baseball team is made up of many smaller stories. These stories take place all over the map—not just in the city a team calls "home." Match the pushpins on these maps to the **TEAM FACTS**, and you will begin to see the story of the Braves unfold!

1 Boston, Massachusetts—*The team played here from 1871 to 1952.*
2 Milwaukee, Wisconsin—*The Braves played here from 1953 to 1965.*
3 Atlanta, Georgia—*The Braves have played here since 1966.*
4 Nitro, West Virginia—*Lew Burdette was born here.*
5 Mobile, Alabama—*Hank Aaron was born here.*
6 New York, New York—*The Braves won the 1957 World Series here.*
7 Texarkana, Texas—*Eddie Mathews was born here.*
8 Portland, Oregon—*Dale Murphy was born here.*
9 DeLand, Florida—*Chipper Jones was born here.*
10 Anaheim, California—*Brian McCann was named the 2010 All-Star Game MVP here.*
11 Sheffield, England—*Harry Wright was born here.*
12 Willemstad, Curaçao—*Andruw Jones was born here.*

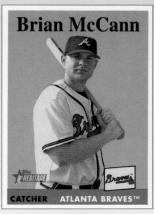

Brian McCann

GLOSSARY

ALL-STAR—A player who is selected to play in baseball's annual All-Star Game.

BIG LEAGUE—The top level of professional baseball.

COMPETITIVE—Talented enough to win.

COMPLETE GAMES—Games started and finished by the same pitcher.

CY YOUNG AWARD—The award given each year to each league's best pitcher.

DECADES—Periods of 10 years; also specific periods, such as the 1950s.

GENERATION—A period of years roughly equal to the time it takes for a person to be born, grow up, and have children.

GOLD GLOVES—The awards given each year to baseball's best fielders.

GRAND SLAMS—Home runs with the bases loaded.

HALL OF FAME—The museum in Cooperstown, New York, where baseball's greatest players are honored.

KNUCKLEBALL—A pitch thrown with no spin, which "wobbles" as it nears home plate.

LOGO—A symbol or design that represents a company or team.

MOST VALUABLE PLAYER (MVP)—The award given each year to each league's top player; an MVP is also selected for the World Series and the All-Star Game.

NATIONAL LEAGUE (NL)—The older of the two major leagues; the NL began play in 1876.

NL EAST—A group of National League teams that play in the eastern part of the country.

NL WEST—A group of National League teams that play in the western part of the country.

PENNANT—A league championship. The term comes from the triangular flag awarded to each season's champion, beginning in the 1870s.

PLATOON—Using more than one player at a position.

PLAYOFFS—The games played after the regular season to determine which teams will advance to the World Series.

ROOKIE OF THE YEAR—The annual award given to each league's best first-year player.

RUNS BATTED IN (RBIs)—A statistic that counts the number of runners a batter drives home.

SAVES—A statistic that counts the number of times a relief pitcher finishes off a close victory for his team.

SHAG—Catch.

SHUTOUT—A game in which one team does not score a run.

STRATEGY—A plan or method for succeeding.

SUMMER OLYMPICS—An international sports competition held every four years.

SUSTAIN—Keep up or continue.

SWITCH-HITTERS—Players who can hit from either side of home plate.

TRADITION—A belief or custom that is handed down from generation to generation.

TRIPLE CROWN—An honor given to a player who leads the league in home runs, batting average, and RBIs.

WORLD SERIES—The world championship series played between the AL and NL pennant winners.

EXTRA INNINGS

TEAM SPIRIT introduces a great way to stay up to date with your team! Visit our **EXTRA INNINGS** link and get connected to the latest and greatest updates. **EXTRA INNINGS** serves as a young reader's ticket to an exclusive web page—with more stories, fun facts, team records, and photos of the Braves. Content is updated during and after each season. The **EXTRA INNINGS** feature also enables readers to send comments and letters to the author! Log onto:

www.norwoodhousepress.com/library.aspx

and click on the tab: **TEAM SPIRIT** to access **EXTRA INNINGS**.

Read all the books in the series to learn more about professional sports. For a complete listing of the baseball, basketball, football, and hockey teams in the **TEAM SPIRIT** series, visit our website at:

www.norwoodhousepress.com/library.aspx

ON THE ROAD

ATLANTA BRAVES
755 Hank Aaron Drive SE
Atlanta, Georgia 30315
(404) 522-7630
atlanta.braves.mlb.com

**NATIONAL BASEBALL
HALL OF FAME AND MUSEUM**
25 Main Street
Cooperstown, New York 13326
(888) 425-5633
www.baseballhalloffame.org

ON THE BOOKSHELF

To learn more about the sport of baseball, look for these books at your library or bookstore:

- Augustyn, Adam (editor). *The Britannica Guide to Baseball*. New York, NY: Rosen Publishing, 2011.

- Dreier, David. *Baseball: How It Works*. North Mankato, MN: Capstone Press, 2010.

- Stewart, Mark. *Ultimate 10: Baseball*. New York, NY: Gareth Stevens Publishing, 2009.

INDEX

ABOUT THE AUTHOR

MARK STEWART has written more than 50 books on baseball and over 150 sports books for kids. He grew up in New York City during the 1960s rooting for the Yankees and Mets, and was lucky enough to meet players from both teams. Mark comes from a family of writers. His grandfather was Sunday Editor of *The New York Times,* and his mother was Articles Editor of *Ladies' Home Journal* and *McCall's.* Mark has profiled hundreds of athletes over the past 25 years. He has also written several books about his native New York and New Jersey, his home today. Mark is a graduate of Duke University, with a degree in history. He lives and works in a home overlooking Sandy Hook, New Jersey. You can contact Mark through the Norwood House Press website.

ML   3/12